Run Fast!

Written by Jo Windsor

This is a little cat.
This little cat can
run fast.

This is a **big** cat. This **big** cat can run fast, too.

Here is a little bird.
This little bird can
run fast.

Here is a **big** bird.
This big bird has long legs.
This big bird can run fast.

Look at this dog.
This dog has
long legs, too.
This dog can
run fast.

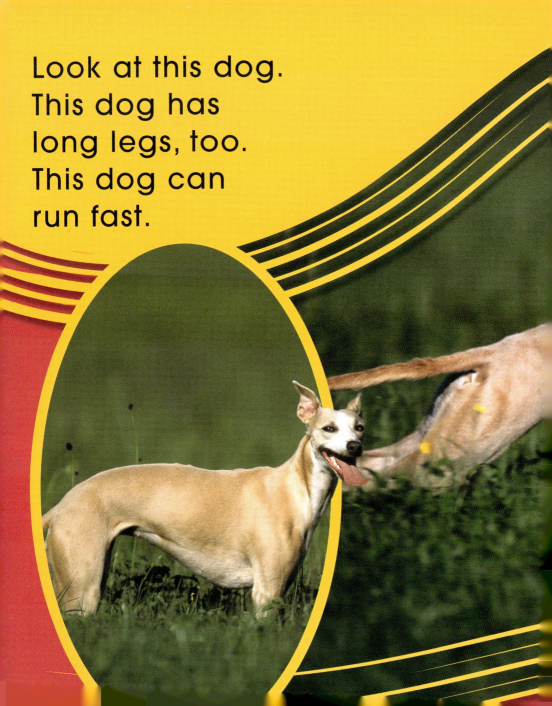

Look at this **big** horse.
This big horse can run fast, too.

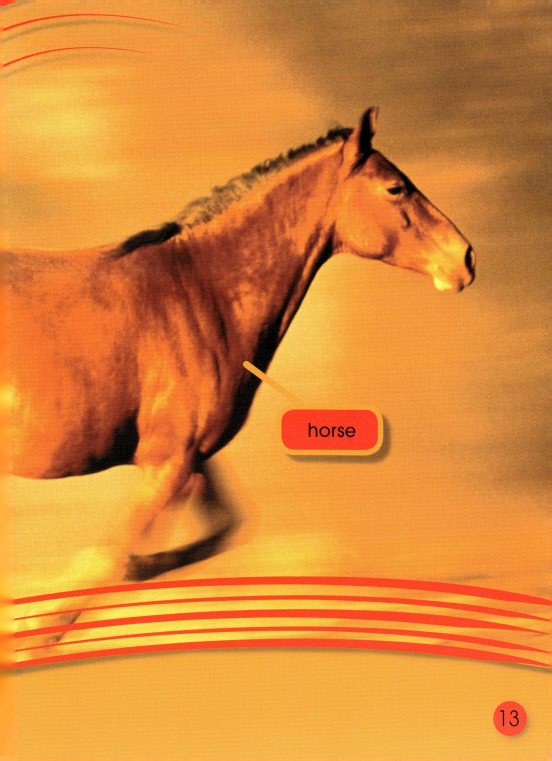

Index

birds....................6, 8
cats....................2, 4
dog..................... 10
horse 12

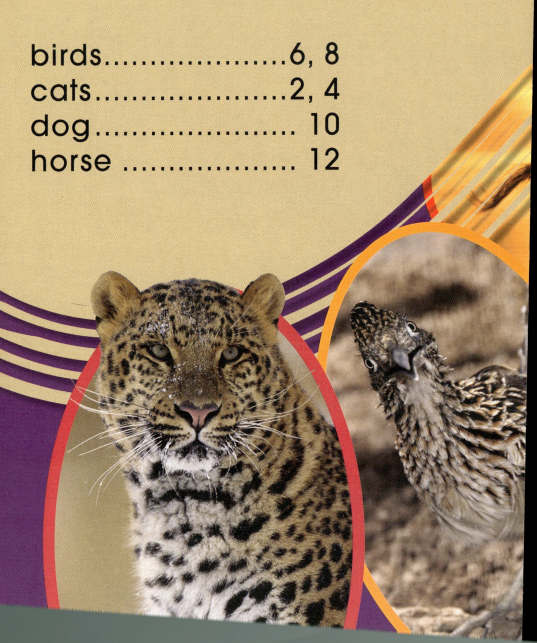

Guide Notes

Title: Run Fast

Stage: Early (1) – Red

Genre: Nonfiction

Approach: Guided Reading

Processes: Thinking Critically, Exploring Language, Processing Information

Written and Visual Focus: Photographs (static images), Index, Labels

Word Count: 77

THINKING CRITICALLY
(sample questions)
- Look at the title and read it to the children.
- Tell them that this book is about animals that can run fast. Ask them which animals they know that can run fast.
- Focus the children's attention on the index. Ask: "What are you going to find out about in this book?"
- If you want to find out about a cat that can run fast, which page would you look on?
- If you want to find out about a horse that can run fast, which page would you look on?
- Why do you think these animals can run fast?
- Why do you think animals might have to run fast?

EXPLORING LANGUAGE

Terminology
Title, cover, photographs, author, photographers

Vocabulary
Interest words: fast, long
High-frequency words: little, too

Print Conventions
Capital letter for sentence beginnings, periods, commas